The
Last Elephant
in
New York City

The
Last Elephant
in
New York City

ELIZABETH KELLY

Epigraph Books
Rhinebeck, New York

The "Visit the Zoo" elephant artwork on the front cover is by Hugh Stevenson. This Works Progress Administration poster is available through the Library of Congress, Prints and Photographs Online Catalog.

CONTENTS

CHAPTER 1

Apartment Tower B obscures what's left of the winter sun. The courtyard is empty. Maxwell Vorsah plugs in the string of lights that arch across his window on the fifth floor of Tower A. The carpeted room is sparse and tidy. There's a wardrobe, a full-length mirror, a few chairs and a cozy bed. He places a hard-to-identify bent aluminum object on the only table next to a handwritten note that says, *Happy 28th. I Love You.*

Maxwell gets to the business of packing the kit he needs for tonight's mission. It takes some doing to get the boom box to fit. He rolls a flashlight and a camera in a dark hooded sweatshirt and stows it in his now oddly rectangular backpack, along with a notebook, two pens, six quarters and a matchbook in a side pocket.

His wife, Jessie, sidesteps out of the kitchenette with what appear to be three baked blobs. One is draped with a shaved carrot star. "I know you're not into birthdays," she says, "but Happy Birthday." She tastes a corner and laugh-coughs biscuit dust. "These are the nuttiest biscuits on the planet."

"I wasn't aiming for biscuit. Those are cookies," he says.

"It's kind of a stretch to call these cookies." When she compares the bent aluminum object on the table to the baked goods in her hands it occurs to her, he made cookies in the shape of elephants for the zoo's elephant that stopped eating four days ago. "That's a cookie cutter?" she asks. "You made a cookie cutter elephant?"

Maxwell fits the cookies into his backpack. He makes room for the cookie cutter, and there's just enough space on top for what he'll need first, headphones and music.

Jessie takes a newspaper-wrapped gift from under the bed. "Dinner's ready whenever. I love you," she says.

The gift is a flashy puffy jacket. "Man! This jacket is fresh," he says.

Jessie has another present, new work boots. He hugs the love of his life, but it's not long before she oozes to the carpet in a good-humored escape from his embrace.

In the low-raking angle of candlelight he sets the table. Dinner for two.

Jessie returns with steamy bowls. "Give it a few. It's way hot," she says.

He risks a scalding spoonful.

"Huugh. Whuugh. This is… wicked-hot soup." He slides his bowl to catch the window draft.

"It's stew," Jessie says.

He tests another bite. "It's good whatever it is. If I hadn't been there that day… when she was taken. No way the poachers would have gotten her out of the park. Alive. And I'm not sure it's the same elephant. It's been twenty years."

"It's her. You'll see," Jessie says.

Jessie is stressed about what, if anything, she can

say to help. "Tonight's the night. Remember it's why we're here. The elephant will remember your voice. She'll remember you said *good girl* to her, over and over. Keep talking to her."

Jessie attempts to lighten the mood with a reenactment of when they first met. She stands. Her delivery is formal and intense. "We have warm drinks in the operations tent. Please follow."

"No way I talk like that," he says.

"That was right on," she says.

* * *

Kakum River, Central Region, Ghana, 1979

Five wildlife rangers greeted the rain-soaked guests. "Is Mr. Maxwell Vorsah here?" Jessie asked.

What luck, the most radiant person he'd ever met wanted to talk to him.

"I'm Maxwell Vorsah."

"Hi. I'm Jessie." He checked her name against his list of guests. "I think I found the elephant that was stolen from here."

"Which one?" he asked.

"Around seventeen years ago. Have there been others?"

"Yes." Maxwell's magnetic smile faded.

"I'm so sorry… I think one of the missing elephants is in a zoo in New York City."

"We have warm drinks in the operations tent. You will need footwear," he said.

* * *

CENTRAL ZOO, NEW YORK, NEW YORK, 1981

After surviving a decades-long down phase, the zoo is ready to go from the "picture-book zoo" that it's been for fifty years to the now more popular style of animal exhibition, the "barless zoo." This will be its second major renovation.

Back in the 1850s, before it was a "picture-book zoo" it was a "menagerie." An informal collection of rare and exotic animals that had appeared in the eight-hundred-acre park in the middle of the city. Gifts and donations from residents on Fifth Avenue.

The animals formally became part of a "zoological garden" and lived in an out-of-use arsenal within the park. The six-acre site was void of pastoral landscape. By the 1930s, the park suffered and life in the cages was unbearable. The zoo closed for renovations and re-opened within a year.

Now all animals have to go before demolition can start. But there are no takers for the ill-tempered, underweight elephant. She has gone from protected contact to the even more isolated status of confined contact, and finally, five years ago, to the roughest designation of all, no contact. Everyone agrees, when this zoo reopens, they will never have another elephant. The last elephant in New York City needs a place to go.

CHAPTER 2

It's time for the uniform for tonight's mission to save the baby elephant captured from Maxwell's home in Ghana on his eighth birthday. Maxwell needs the forest-green shirt in the wardrobe. He irons it, careful not to singe the embroidery that says Central Zoo.

"Shirt looks good," Jessie says.

He nods yes, it certainly does look good. "If I get the night watch job…"

"*When* you get the night watch job," Jessie interrupts. "Come on, say it."

He scrunches into yuck-face.

"You'll get the job. You know elephants. You already work at the zoo with the hippos. The zoo needs graveyard shifts covered for the holidays. And no one's lining up to work with a troubled ten-thousand-pound animal."

"Nine thousand," he says.

"Oh, wow. She's down to nine thousand?"

"Maybe even less," he says.

"Hippos like it when you read to them." Jessie hands Maxwell his dictionary. "No way this fits in your backpack. You'll have ten hours to work with her before the morning keeper shows up. Who's on for the early shift?"

It's not good news. "Roy," he says.

"Bummer. Maybe with all the snow that's about to bury the city he won't get there?"

"He'll show up. Has to." Maxwell checks his watch. "I can crank out the dishes."

"Two bowls. A couple of spoons. I've got it," she says.

The backpack makes an awkward mess of the new jacket. He has one last thing to say before he leaves. "A bit bunchy?"

* * *

The narrow hallway is littered with sand and salt tracked in by residents. Maxwell secures both locks and crunches down five flights. The bus screeches and pre-blizzard tire chains rattle as his ride approaches. He checks a pocket for bus fare and comes up with one key and a few almonds, but no quarters. He digs around because he's sure he put the coins somewhere.

Maxwell greets the driver and has his choice of rows. He picks a window seat, considers his reflection and mouths, *Yeah man, this jacket is fresh*. He thinks back to the last time he saw his dad, on his eighth birthday. He presses fast forward on the cassette. Stop. Play. Fast forward. It lands at almost the right spot. Awash in rhythm, his head and shoulders collapse and rebuild. He's into his tunes. Passengers make their way down Fifth Avenue. Sporadic holiday lights sparkle in building entrances and apartment windows.

* * *

In the 1930s, as mahogany logging swept through the Central Region, a handful of people dedicated themselves to protecting the animals. Maxwell's dad was one of the best trackers of the most endangered large animals. He worked month-long shifts along the Kakum River and always returned with stories about elephants. Maxwell believed so many terrible things happened because his birthday wish was to see where the elephants lived. The best spots were on opposite sides of the ninety-two-thousand-eight-hundred-acre forest reserve. From the final favorite spot, they saw blood.

Maxwell followed his dad into the forest because his dad was certain an elephant had hidden her calf before she was killed. They found the super-cute baby, all snuggled up and sad. It took an hour to drag her to the road and heave her into the truck. Maxwell learned how to start an IV. He was told to ride with the elephant, hold the fluids above her heart, keep covered and stay low, a lot for an eight-year-old to handle.

They ran out of gas on the way to the elephant nursery. The elephant passed out and Maxwell was pinned when they got jacked by two trucks. Ivory wasn't enough. The poachers wanted the calf too. Maxwell buried himself and the elephant in everything he could scrounge. But then the elephant rumbled, which was good and bad.

It meant the elephant was awake and feeling better. But seconds later, there were three guns pointed at Maxwell. One of the poachers was concerned about the IV and demanded that father or son, whoever could keep the elephant alive longer, come with them.

"Son. You did well here. This is not your fault. Promise to find this elephant. She is family." This was the last time Maxwell saw his dad. Maxwell walked through the night-forest to the elephant nursery to tell his dad's best friends what had happened.

CHAPTER 3

NEW YORK, NEW YORK, DECEMBER 1981

The bus hits traffic. Maxwell hops off at the next stop and tests the weight and fit of his prized new boots. One lace needs adjustment. He replaces his jacket with the *I LOVE NY* sweatshirt and arranges his backpack. It's a clearer stretch, fewer traffic lights on the uneven hexagonal pavers that flank the park wall. He sets off at an easy jog. Street signs count down fifteen blocks south. Flakes of snow make their way to earth.

Maxwell stops at the Central Zoo maintenance entrance. He has the key he needs to unlock the first gate. The cast iron street lamp barely sheds light on this rescue mission. He checks the flashlight. On. Off. All systems go. He stops in the courtyard to take a picture of the granite eagles that guard the brick clock tower.

The companionship of hippos is what he needs to calm his nerves, so he visits their barn. He greets his good-humored crew. "What's up, farty friends? I'm going to check out that elephant. I'll report back if it's really her."

There's a security officer he needs to avoid. Predictable rounds make it easy. Maxwell slips out of the hippo barn and advances through the zoo. The predator cats are awake and curious. Polar bear eyes glow in the center of the courtyard. Maxwell comforts the frustrated bear. "You're a cool bear. Major snow tonight. Big fun, roll and scrub around in it. See you in the morning."

Maxwell reviews the top things on his mind on his way to the elephant. He has to get into the barn. He needs to stabilize her mind… get her to eat… get the night watch job. The revolving gate into the yard is locked. No big deal. He scales the wall, drops into the enclosure and lands in an antiseptic footbath. "Aw, man! Not the new boots."

He begins with a check of the outdoor elephant yard and takes a photo of an ice shelf on a crushed plastic barrel. Click. He takes another picture of the long-abandoned play thing and places a cookie on top. After a year working at the zoo, Maxwell knows where to find the spare key to get into the elephant barn.

His first stop inside is the feed room. He scans for resources and then washes his hands. There's a staff corner with three lockers and a blue beach chair propped against a chrome and vinyl table. And a cooler filled with cabbages and a stack of what looks to be very undesirable bricks of oats. There's a note taped to the people fridge. WARNING! DANGEROUS ANIMAL. NO CONTACT. The other fridge is for all the elephant medications. Buckets and supplements line the walls and shelves.

A complicated bundle of keys hangs from a mug hook. He sorts until he finds the one he needs for the massive metal door that gets him into the holding area. Almost there, it clanks open and he finally sees the elephant. She rocks from side to side, over and over, in the farthest corner of her house. Beyond human range, the elephant rumbles at an infrasonic fourteen hertz. No elephants reply.

CHAPTER 4

Streetlight from the barred window casts rays over damp cinder walls. Chains drag across concrete. An underweight elephant positions her mangled feet in slivers of light. The elephant's pain is obvious. She stops at chain's end.

The holding area floor is painted with three zones. The green zone is the safe zone, the area believed to be beyond the reach of the animal, plus some. Everyone knows no one walks in the yellow striped caution zone.

The red zone is the danger zone, the area within reach of the animal.

Maxwell sets his kit in the safe zone and sits on the concrete. "Good girl. Do you remember me?" The elephant keeps her distance and her back turned. To get a sense of the animal's physical condition Maxwell shines his flashlight on a fleshy hind foot. "Concrete is hard on the feet. Do you remember Africa? Is it really you? Good girl. Good girl."

The metallic sound of the jangly keys distresses the elephant when he stands. She scrapes a wound along a wall. It's devastating to see the self-destructive behavior. "Ouch. Don't do that. You're a good elephant."

To begin the process of desensitizing her to at least one disruptive sound, he shakes the loud mess of keys while he repeats kind words. "Good elephant. Be cool with the jangle. Zone in on good. Tune out the rest. Around here that's a lot. You're going to get out of here. Good elephant."

The good elephant turns to a three-quarter view. "Keys are good," he whispers. She dials into his words. "Good girl." He jangles the keys. "Keys are your ticket out of here. Check out how many we already have. It's hard to tell with you way back there. My hands will know for sure if it's really you. Barely alive, unsound mind… if you fade away in this cage, no matter your form. Flesh or skeleton, I'm here to help. Good girl."

Despite the shackles, she steps forward, toward the new guy. Every time the elephant moves, chains drag. "Do you remember me?" The elephant's head droops. Maxwell steps closer to the painted line between caution and danger. "Do you remember your home? I found your mother. Way later. All flat and returned to earth. I promised the scattered bones I'd find you. Do you remember? We all ended up with guns to our heads."

The elephant disengages. She's stuck in retreat mode, but Maxwell wants her to move closer. With an ultra-efficient gesture, he indicates to the elephant that he also hears the annoying mechanical hum of the heating system. He gets her attention when he removes all instruments of time. His watch goes into his backpack, and he unplugs the ticking wall clock in the holding area.

Maxwell gets cookie number two. "You have to eat. Good elephant." They make eye contact. "They stopped trying to get you to go out to the yard, but go outside, even if it's cold. I left something out there for you. Try to get your heart rate up and get in a good workout." She zones out on the streaks of tungsten light that seep in from her window.

* * *

Elephant Dream

The captive elephant invents a way out of her cage. She positions her mangled feet in the slivers of light. The elephant transforms into a skeleton and slips her chains. Most bones pass through the bars. Clonk. Some need to rotate a few degrees, and so on. The skull is tricky. Piece by piece, she escapes. The elephant skeleton reassembles outside the cage. Clicketty, clackitty, she heads straight for an exit.

End Elephant Dream

* * *

Maxwell goes to the feed room and returns with the beach chair. It creaks when he sets it up in the caution zone. "Sketchy chair. Snow's kicking out there. Are we going to get a full-on blizzard?" He offers her the second cookie but she refuses to budge. The cookie wiggles. "Here. Eat it. It's for you. It's a cookie." Impossible to resist, the word *cookie* does the trick. She approaches the bars. But she still has no appetite, so he tucks the cookie into the woven plastic chair.

"Do people read to you? Let's give it a try. First, I'll write you a note." Pen click on. Pen click off. He needs a few more seconds to decide what to write. Pen click on. Four lines later, he's finished with the short note. He folds it like a fan and tucks it into the chair. "I've got to score the night watch job. Interview's in the morning at seven with Roy. Pretend we just met."

Maxwell hunts for every light switch in the barn. He tests what order he'll work the switches, two at a time for some lights. It gets darker. The elephant hobbles closer. "Tune out the chains. Good girl. Where's the switch for that light?" He finds it. All the lights are off, and he's almost invisible with his hood up and back turned.

Shackles collide. "That's every light I can find. But it's never dark dark in the city. And it's only quiet when it snows."

He drops to the floor for a quick set of super-impressive pushups. The elephant is intrigued. She rumbles, then retreats to the window. "You can't slide anything past family, so watch what you rumble." She'd prefer to evaluate the new guy from forty feet away, mostly with sound and scent, but here, stuck in this cage, eighteen feet is the maximum distance.

The elephant turns her head. It looks like she has a question. Something like, *You hear what I rumble?* He's pretty sure he knows that look. "Yeah, that's right. We're family."

He whistles and strikes a match. The elephant adjusts her angle to align with the diminutive flame. Stabilized, her head is calm, no weaving or repetitive behaviors. Things are going well. Maxwell adjusts his posture, steps into the danger zone, reaches through the bars and touches the elephant. "I'm one hundred percent, it's you. How did you get here? To this exact spot? Land? Sea? Air? Did you go on a train? Nothing's more major than shipping an elephant, but we can't find any records. Where were you before this? Performing? Breeding? I have so many questions. We know who took you. But who shipped you?"

He gets the stash of almonds from a pocket and pings one into the cage. The elephant moves toward the treat. He adjusts his aim to get the rest to scatter on the floor. She calculates landing sounds and shuffles around in the dark to find the tiny almonds. It's not nearly enough calories for her to survive, but any appetite is a good sign.

Click, he gets a once-in-a-lifetime photo of her vapor in the dark cage. The rejuvenated elephant likes the camera and approaches the bars as if the chains don't exist. "You like cameras? I like cameras too. It might be way too dark for any of these to come out, but who knows?"

Maxwell puts the camera away and goes to the dictionary for tonight's word. He flips pages and mutters. "L, M, N. Got it. Tonight's word is *night*. It means *darkness between one day and the next*. I'll be here with you every darkness between one day and the next."

These are her last days if she doesn't eat. To get her to focus on the cookie, he shines his flashlight on the beach chair. But it's not the cookie that gets her attention. "What are you looking at?" He offers her the see-through aluminum object. "The cookie cutter? Be cool. Here. Check it out. See what you can do with it. Needs some work."

Maxwell sweeps his hands across her arthritic elbow while she inspects and then crushes the bent aluminum elephant-cookie-cutter project. Three massive bars forward, he presses his hands into to her contact-deprived head and supports what weight she allows. "Big beautiful animal. I'm so sorry." The reunion is too intense. She breaks away but stays near the bars. She makes a slow circle with her head, and then her trunk reaches through the bars and rests on his shoulder. It's not possible to know for sure, but it appears the elephant remembers him, and forgives him.

He cries. "Poor little animal. Did you see what they did to your mother? I hope not." In search of a footrest and a break to pull himself together, he goes to the feed room and returns with an empty bucket and flips it upside down. "Graveyard shift deluxe lounge in the works. No one knows what happened to my father. Maybe you do? We can't find him."

Maxwell flaps the fanned note along the bars. The elephant tilts her head toward the unusual sound. "Good girl." He unfolds and reads the note. "Poor elephant. You have nothing earthy. So few interesting things. And you're beyond the range of other elephants." She moves as close to him as the bars allow. "We'll return to a grassy lowland."

He offers her the cookie again. "Eat cookies." She considers the instruction. *Eat cookies* is fun compared to lots of other demands she's endured. "It has tons of nuts." She reacts to the word *nuts*. She shifts her weight and raises her right front leg as high as she can. "Oh. Big cutie. You don't have to do that. This cookie is for you. Here. Eat."

She takes the treat and is careful not to break it. Under the cage window with the bars that guard the glass that protects her from the world, the elephant tastes the tiniest bit. Her new night handler tells her to finish the cookie. She obeys.

"You must have watched so many storms from that window." He moves the chair and footrest to the exact spot, in the danger zone, where he plans to settle in for a few hours. He keeps talking to the lonely elephant.

"Jessie gave me this sweatshirt. She's from here, born in this city. She grew up a mile away. She's a total trouper about our apartment. Our radiators hiss but don't produce much heat. We have a small table next to a window. It's where I make things like the cookie cutter you crushed. Jessie's a researcher. She works from home a lot, or in libraries. She likes to sweep, not into irons, she's a really good cook. You met her once. A long time ago, back when you were the Queen of the Zoo."

CHAPTER 5

CENTRAL ZOO, NEW YORK CITY, JUNE 1965

A class trip of girls with plaid pinafores covered by a tapestry of overcoats, mostly pink, skipped across hexagonal pavers. The city park was in bloom. The group arrived at the main entrance of the Central Zoo. Eleven little princesses organized into a line from shortest to tallest. Two parent chaperones did a head count.

The teacher, Miss Emmy, said, "Girls. Girls! Huddle in, little princesses. Is everyone ready to meet the animals?" All the girls confirm *Yes!* With a delicate finger to her lips, Miss Emmy said, "Soft voices with the animals, and no running. We have a special pass to meet the Queen of the Zoo, Loxodonta africana. Does anyone know what a Loxodonta africana is?" No girls knew the answer. The parent chaperones also came up with nothing.

Miss Emmy explained, "Loxodonta africana is the Latin name for African elephant. Elephants have excellent memory." The small group buzzed with excitement. They halted at the brick clock tower when Miss Emmy signaled stop. "Stay close. But if anyone gets separated, please meet here. Don't wander around." Miss Emmy pointed to a plank that indicated left turn and asked the group, "Who can read this sign?"

"Hippo barn," three girls hollered. They already knew they were correct.

"How many hippos live there?" one of them asked.

"Good question. Four hippos," Miss Emmy said. She pointed to the plank that indicated right turn and said, "Raise your hands this time. Who can read this sign?" All the girls raised a hand, some reached impossibly high. Jessie's hand was raised but only half-high, somewhere near her ear. Jessie was more into the rhinestone rainbow on her denim jacket than answering this easy question. "Jessica," Miss Emmy said.

"Elephant barn."

"That's correct, elephant barn," Miss Emmy said.

The group made their way down the path to the elephant barn. The most confident girls skipped, but only a few times so they wouldn't get in trouble. "Elephants are social with strong family bonds," Miss Emmy said. "They can communicate over great distances." Miss Emmy gestured what low-frequency sound waves might look like. "With low-frequency sound waves in a language beyond human range. It's called infrasound. Sometimes elephants rumble as low as fourteen hertz. Around twenty hertz is the lowest sound wave humans can sense."

The level of student attentiveness was moderate, actually, considerably less. Never mind, the teacher kept at it. "Giraffes communicate with infrasound too. A sound wave is when compression and refraction move a vibration through an elastic medium, like air." The current level of interest in whatever it was the teacher was going on about was now zero percent.

A leopard called attention to the abundant teaching tools available in the zoo. Miss Emmy reconnected with her students. "Who wants to talk to an elephant?" Everyone raised a hand.

They arrived at the elephant yard. "We have a special pass that gets us into the barn. Not just the yard. Let's meet the Queen of the Zoo."

"How many elephants live here?" Jessie asked.

"Just one," Miss Emmy said.

The group collected at the revolving gate. Miss Emmy went through first and demonstrated how to step into the blue-green antiseptic footbath. "Make sure you get it on all the edges of your shoes." The elephant yard was dreary. She took her post at the corner of the barn. "One at a time. Come through the revolving gate, and step in the footbath. Then, line up next to me. Who wants to go first?" No one wanted to go first. A chaperone selected a girl.

The reluctant student said, "Eww. Do I have to step in it?"

"Yes. So that our feet don't bring in microbes that can make the elephant sick," Miss Emmy said. The student plastered herself to her teacher's side. Jessie went through next. She stepped in the footbath and lined up near her teacher, but not exactly next to anyone.

Miss Emmy checked her watch. "We are way behind schedule." While the rest of the group decided who would be next, the most anxious girl sprung through the barrier.

The little overcoats were luminescent against the limestone wall. A chaperone sneezed into her elbow. "Excuse me. Allergies," she said. She removed lint from her pocket and told her colleague, "Washing machine obliterated a tissue."

They filtered into the dark interior, where the one elephant lived. The feed room was to the left of the group. Green paint on the floor delineated the safe zone. The yellow caution zone, the red danger zone, and the cage were to the right. Everyone turned toward the bars.

The young morning keeper, Roy, circled the petrified group. "The danger zone is everywhere the elephant can reach." He stomped on the hard line between the safe zone and the caution zone. "Don't mess with this line. That window's her favorite spot." The phone rang in the feed room. "I've got to get that. Who's in charge of the group?"

"I am, sir," Miss Emmy said.

"No one goes out of the green area." Roy left the group unsupervised.

* * *

An underweight elephant faced a wall in her concrete cage. A slice of light from a window cast a mesmerizing pattern across her hide. The colossal animal was lifeless.

"Does she move?" Jessie asked.

"She has nowhere to go," Miss Emmy said.

"This is not a good house," Jessie whispered.

"It's dreadful," Miss Emmy said.

The elephant shifted her weight and shackles collided. Miss Emmy tried to lift the mood. "She's turning. She's wants to say hello. Look. She's so beautiful."

The elephant surveyed today's audience. Out of eleven girls and three grown-ups, it was low-profile Jessie who won the attention of the Queen of the Zoo. Miss Emmy was happy for this young lady's extraordinary moment. "Jessica. Look at that! The elephant is pointing to you." The rest of the group clumped together, back row on tiptoes.

Jessie checked that her feet were in the green zone, but didn't retreat with the group.

Miss Emmy surprised her with a suggestion. "How about moving a little closer to the elephant?" Jessie waited for instructions from the biggest, saddest, most amazing animal she'd ever met. The elephant lowered her head in a gentle, friendly manner, so Jessie took a step forward. The elephant adjusted her position to improve the sight line. They made eye contact.

"What's it like? So close to a Loxodonta africana," Miss Emmy asked.

Instead of an answer, Jessie had two questions. "This is the elephant's whole house? Forever?" The elephant retreated when she heard the morning keeper's keys, so Jessie did the same.

CHAPTER 6

CENTRAL ZOO, NEW YORK CITY, DECEMBER 1981

Maxwell asks the dying elephant, "Do you remember a class trip with a special pass? Somehow you asked Jessie to help you find your family. She never forgot you. In high school she started trying to figure out where you came from. It's hard to find info on captured wild animals. A month after she graduated from university she showed up in Ghana with news."

The elephant is calm. She likes night watch story time. He makes chair and bucket adjustments and keeps talking to her. "Some of the guests were expecting more of an open-plains safari. With all the heavy rain they barely left their tents. Except Jessie. She didn't love the conditions, but she handled it. Even the stuff she called peanut-butter mud. She fell asleep outside by the fire on the last night. First guest ever to sleep outside. I sat with her. Guns within reach. I got the coffee started in the morning. When she woke up, she said something like, wow, that smells good. Then she asked if I'd come to New York with her."

Maxwell inspects his new boots. "Check these out. Birthday present. I never make wishes anymore. But Jessie said this year I had to ask for at least one thing she could wrap." He loosens the laces. "Jessie worked with us in the park for ten weeks, and then we flew to New York. I needed resident status to qualify for the job with the hippos. She said she was the luckiest woman on earth to get to marry me. We moved into a five-flight walk-up. It's a huge building with elevators but our line's always out. We've got a comfortable bed. Windows that open." He reaches into the cage. The elephant isn't within range.

* * *

Maxwell wakes at two o'clock and rolls a luminous cabbage to the elephant's shackled feet. She eats. He wakes at three and rolls another cabbage into the cage. He wakes at four and blasts the overhead lights. They buzz. The elephant squints and tosses her head. She's in a dark mood. "No matter what, we're family. You're going to get out of here. Time for another cookie." The elephant tilts her troubled head toward the artificial sound of the lights. "They buzz like that in the hippo barn too, when they've been off and it's cold." The elephant drops a massive poop by the cage door. Some of it lands in the danger zone.

He lights a match. "Good signs are gross. I can reach some of that with a shovel. Where's the muck shovel?" He returns with the shovel of all shovels. "Well! I guess this is The Shovel. Seriously? Look at the size of this thing." He evaluates the sloppy chore and flashes the opposite of his magnetic smile. He gets the boom box and asks, "Do you like music? Have you ever seen a boom box as sweet as this?"

He tunes the dial. The first radio station that comes in is holiday music. The next best reception is another station with more holiday music. "*Ba rump*? What's up with holiday music?" He adjusts the dial until he finds what he's looking for and gets to mucking. The first scoop drips into the muck bucket. Three more shovels of what he can reach from outside the bars, and the danger zone is smeared more than cleared. He goes for the high-pressure hose.

The elephant freaks out and slams against the wall. "Shhh. Easy. It's okay. Shhh. You know what? We'll leave it." He replaces the hose in a tidy coil, turns the lights off again, and settles back into the creaky beach chair. "It helps to have something to look forward to. If I get the night watch job…. *when* I get the job, we'll go on imaginary adventures in the park. When it's hot, we'll lounge in Sheep Meadow with fresh air and shade trees. We'll stretch our legs and get in a good workout." He strikes a match and whistles. Chains drag. Carpeted in fresh snow, the city is quiet. They fall asleep.

CHAPTER 7

The light on this unpolished morning signals the elephant. After so many years of the same routine, she knows it's time for a shift change. Maxwell is still asleep, so she blasts a fart at him. "Oh, man! Eat a fart. Thanks for that." He warms his hands, checks his watch, and gets into hustle mode.

"Interview's in half an hour." He resets the clock, tick, tick. He returns the chair and bucket to the feed room and gets the barn in order. The elephant watches his efficient movements. He points to the unauthorized object in the elephant's possession. She passes him the crushed cookie cutter.

Maxwell replaces his sweatshirt with his new jacket and readies to greet Roy in the yard. Waist-deep snow makes it impossible to return the spare barn key to its hiding spot without tracks, so he tucks the key away for now. Roy stomps and shakes accumulated snow. Maxwell extends a hand, but Roy's in a bad mood and doesn't reciprocate.

"Let's get inside," Roy barks. "City's shut down. Worst I've ever seen it. How'd you get here before me? If it weren't for this damned elephant I'd be in bed. You're here for the night watch job? The director wants to get her through the holidays. You're from over in hippo barn. Do you know anything about elephants?"

"Yes," Maxwell says.

"What's with that hideous jacket?" Roy knows exactly which key he needs to unlock the holding area door. "Ready?" he asks.

There's a sense of well-being in the barn. Roy is surprised by the elephant's healthy posture and positive reaction to a new person. "That's kind of different," he says. "Should have seen her yesterday for a class trip. What a nightmare. Seeing her now… I wonder."

Roy chucks the bundle of keys at the interviewee. "Can I count on you to show up on time?"

"Yes," Maxwell says.

"Her next weigh-in is in two weeks if she makes it that long."

"She'll make it," Maxwell says.

"Night watch job's yours if you're up for it. It's temporary. Just through the holidays. Feed and water, that's it. No contact."

Mission accomplished, Maxwell bombards the polar bear with playful snowballs on his way to the exit. "Good bear." The bear plows through a shoulder-high drift.

CHAPTER 8

The last elephant in New York City has one final chance. "Demolish the brick!" All parties agree, do whatever it takes to get the elephant out of the cage. But many measurements later, there's no consensus on how. It's cold, and the sledgehammer crew know the wall with the window is the weak spot. They take turns and get the wall down faster than anyone imagined possible. They hang around in case there's something else to get out of the way of the elephant.

Everyone hopes the elephant will load onto a special truck and she'll make it to a place with soft earth and other elephants. Twenty-five people wish for the elephant's last chance to make it by end of day. The zoo director, the vet, one city representative, one park ranger, two police officers, two human-interest press passes, three sledge-hammerers, four zoo staff, four high-level executives and six lawyers all chat while they wait. No friends and family are allowed, in case things go wrong. The radios buzz. The special truck is here!

The driver maneuvers the custom trailer. No mirror does as fine a job as the driver's head out the window. Right hand down. Left hand down. Frigid air reddens his face. "How about parking over there by the eagles?" the director asks. The director points to the granite eagles that guard the clock tower, next to where the polar bear used to live. The driver shakes his head, no.

Roy takes over and tells the driver to park wherever he thinks is best. Roy informs the tense group, "I'll come through with the dangerous elephant. From over there. To here. Everyone huddle up on the far side of the courtyard. No photos." The group obeys.

Chains drag. The elephant appears. Roy's in the lead. Maxwell and two staff follow with sticks. The elephant shrinks in the intense sun. This isn't the way she came into the zoo all those years ago. Overwhelmed, she approaches the ramp and stops. The elephant goes to the ground. Roy commands, "Up! Up! Come on. You're so close. Come on! Up!" The elephant does not move. Ten minutes pass, fifteen minutes, half an hour, everyone is miserable.

The zoo director takes the vet aside, away from the crowd. They convene in front of the trailer. The director asks the vet, "It's been an hour, what do we do?"

"I don't know," the vet says.

"An anonymous donor paid to get her to California. All we have to do is get her on that truck." The director perches on the bumper and glosses over the backup plan. "If she doesn't get up, I'll clear as many people as I can. Tractor's behind the barn. If anything happens to Roy, that guy over there is the go-to." The director points to Maxwell.

"Why him?"

"Don't know what it is but he's good with that elephant." The director checks his elegant watch. "Let's give this a few more minutes. Remember the blizzard? That was the elephant's best night in who knows how long?"

The driver drops out of his command station at the wheel. "The elephant does. And by the way, those are falcons, not eagles," he says. The driver goes straight for Maxwell and asks, "Can you get her up?" The elephant is flat on her side.

"Yes," Maxwell says.

The driver presses, "Do it now."

Maxwell goes to her and slides his hands under her ear. "You're a good elephant. I will say your favorite word. When I say your favorite word, no matter how hard it is, get up and onto the truck. This is your ride out of here. It's now or never. Get on the truck. Good girl." He lifts what weight he can and repeats the instructions. "When I say your favorite word, stand. And get on the truck."

Maxwell disperses the pack of people and suggests positions around the perimeter as random as possible. "Who has a camera?" he asks. Everyone raises a hand. "Take as many pictures as you like. She loves cameras. We need to get her up." All the cameras come out and the elephant flaps her tail. Click, click, she lifts her head.

Maxwell is ready. "Good girl. Here we go. Cookie!" The elephant inhales, exhales, shifts weight, sways, then rocks, and gets caught in an unnatural seated position. Everyone encourages her. She stands and greets today's audience.

Roy lobs a question at the vet. "When's the last time she greeted an audience like that?"

The elephant points to a person with a pink press pass. The reporter steps forward and does her best to interpret the magnificent elephant's message. "Yes. I'll share your story," she says to the elephant.

The elephant follows Maxwell onto the truck. The driver introduces himself to Maxwell. "Hey, I'm Otto."

"I'm Maxwell."

"How much does she weigh?"

"Nine thousand three-hundred pounds. Give or take fifty," Maxwell says.

"Are you up for a road trip? We need to leave ten minutes ago."

"How many days?"

"With this load? Don't know. I'm guessing five," Otto says.

"I'll get my knapsack. Be right back."

"What's a knapsack?"

Maxwell runs to the barn and returns. "I grabbed a whole bunch of tranqs."

Otto secures the ramp and points to the shotgun rack. "And we've got those," he says.

"Do we stop on the way?" Maxwell asks.

"Straight through. There's three, maybe four places I can pull this custom rig over. And we don't want to get weighed. We'll have a couple of safety snoozes. Cab sleeps one. We'll stop to feed and water the elephant." Otto shows Maxwell the coolers strapped behind the compact sleeping cab. One cooler is for food, and the other is for drinks. There's a six-pack of beer on ice and an equal number of cranberry juices.

Otto checks his mirrors and pops in a cassette, classic rock. He calculates the load-weight by feel and avoids the brick pile from the recently demolished segment of the zoo's outermost wall. Otto backs the Queen of the Zoo onto Fifth Avenue. He signals the police escort he's ready to roll. Otto listens but can't make out what the cop says over the radio. It appears they get the go-ahead for lights and sirens.

They make their way toward the tunnel. A second

police escort joins them, and then another. Otto stops the convoy two blocks east of the tunnel entrance. He hollers to the cops, "I need a straight shot into the tunnel. Both lanes." Otto kicks a boot onto the dashboard and prepares to chill. "This'll take a while." He points to the CB radio. "Mostly I go by Night Otter."

"Night Otter? That's your handle? You picked Night Otter?"

"My brother was messing around on the radio one night, and it stuck," Otto says.

"Where are we headed?"

"West."

It's only a couple of minutes before a cop bangs a flashlight on the side of the trailer. The noise upsets the elephant. The cop approaches the driver's window and asks, "Can I take a picture?"

"Go for it," Maxwell says. The cop climbs the wheel well, click.

"How much does it weigh?" the cop asks. Otto knows exactly how much his load weighs, but he shrugs instead of answering. "Thought it'd take a lot longer but we got the go-ahead. Tunnel is clear. I'll go first. Lights and sirens."

"Ten miles an hour. Lights. No sirens in the tunnel," Otto says.

* * *

They creep under the river and resurface at the toll both. Otto says what everyone's thinking.

"No way we fit through there."

The MTA has an alternate route ready, and the special trailer is directed around the tolls. The truck makes a seismic shift. Otto needs to do something to get the elephant to settle. He brakes firm enough to get her a little unbalanced, then he accelerates. It works. They pick up a state trooper who waves hello, and then does a somewhat obnoxious U-turn at the Pennsylvania border. The interstate is wide open. Otto slaps the fuzz buster on the dash.

CHAPTER 9

Road trip, U.S.A., February 1983

Mile by mile, they drag weight through the night. Five hours into the trip, Otto wakes Maxwell.

"There's a stop coming up. It has a phone," he says. They unfurl from the truck.

Maxwell calls Jessie. No answer. Maxwell refreshes in the rest stop sink and buys jugs of water. The truck rattles. He runs to the trailer. "Easy. Good girl. Hello, elephant. Thirsty?" he asks. She drinks two gallons of water and munches an oat brick.

"Let's roll," Otto says.

Otto checks the mirrors and engages a creeper gear. He eases back onto the interstate and gets the rig up to cruise speed, seventy miles per hour, and then he drops a bomb. "Jessie put this all together."

"Man! What?"

"I transport exotics, mostly circuses and collectors. Logistically, elephants and giraffes are tough, but I think they kind of like some parts of life on the road. I wouldn't do it otherwise. Look. I know it's not pasture and freedom but it's what I do. If not me, someone else. I drive big and dangerous animals. As long as it's not to someplace worse."

"What does Jessie have to do with this?"

"Everything. She charmed a few teamsters and they told her to find the Night Otter. I was asleep on a round hay bale near Chicago. She smiled, shook my hand, and thanked me for my time with a hundred bucks. She asked two questions. Can I get a truck that can handle an African elephant? And, how much will it cost for me to be on call for an elephant emergency? Look, man. I don't know how she paid for all of it. But I've never gotten a tunnel cleared and around a toll so fast. And this isn't my first elephant. I was in Atlanta when I got word it was go-time. I told her I could be there by five the next day. But to get that size animal off the island of Manhattan, we'd need an almost impossible list of things to happen. The police escort from the zoo was mostly just for fun. She got it all done. Brick walls down, tunnel cleared, and a place to go."

"How much does this transport cost?"

"Not much. Fuel cost. Plus, three nights in a seaside hotel after I deliver the animal. I'm so down for fresh sheets, hot shower, feet up, and cracking all six frosties in the cooler."

* * *

Maxwell and Otto take turns with music selection and stop a few more times for food and water. One stop is for rest. Otto tosses Maxwell a sleeping bag. Maxwell greets his big friend in the trailer and selects his snooze spot. It's definitely in the danger zone. At four in the morning, Otto knocks on an aluminum panel and announces, "On the road in ten." Maxwell tends to the elephant and visits the dank roadside bathroom. The vending machine has one thing for elephants. He buys all the nuts.

"So, what's up with you? Where're you from?" Otto asks.

"Ghana."

"Africa? How'd you end up in New York?"

"Long story."

"Well. We've got three hundred miles."

* * *

The Sierra Nevada mountains are in distant sight, and Maxwell has the perfect song ready for when they hit the flattest and widest spot to cross the California border. But it's another two hours, and Maxwell falls asleep before they arrive at the large animal hideout. Otto gears the truck down to a steady fifteen miles an hour. He skims into a parking lot with such ease it appears he must have done this maneuver before.

Otto elbows Maxwell. "Wait in the truck. I'll find out where to unload. If anyone asks what's up, don't say anything. Not even to the elephant." Otto leaves the truck running.

When he's back from the office he slaps a stack of paper on the dash. "This is some shady paperwork," he says. "But we're in. The elephants are up that way." The live cargo shifts as they haul the last elephant from New York City up the hill. She trumpets. An elephant trumpets back.

END

Two Elephants
Work Out

ELIZABETH KELLY

CENTRAL PARK, NEW YORK, 1981

As the sun rises over the rooftops of the white-glove buildings along the eastern boundary of Sheep Meadow, an elephant skeleton wanders into the park. Not fixed in time or form, he's an ancestral guardian that comes to the aid of animals in distress. His name is Africa.

He selects his spot next to the mature tree with the best view. A second elephant skeleton speed-walks in. Her name is Zoo.

"How was traffic from the zoo?" Africa asks.

Zoo is winded. "Light today. I'm the only elephant on the road," she says.

Zoo sets up at an awkward distance about an acre away. The skeletons rattle every time they move.

Possessions not typical of an elephant appear out of nowhere. Zoo arranges her yellow-striped hula hoop, water bottle, ticking wall clock, and jangly keys in a space-claiming way.

Zoo misjudges how loud she needs to be to communicate. She hollers across the meadow. "Don't let me forget where I put those keys! Sorry. Way too loud. Right? It's been so long since I talked to other elephants. What time did'ya get here?"

Africa's not sure how to answer questions about time, so he turns away from her. With a well-practiced toss, she rolls her hula hoop across the grassy field. In life, elephants can't see color, but in skeleton form, they do. The yellow is vivid and it gets Africa's attention. He's nimble and spins around with ease. Africa is quick to pick up Zoo's unusual way of squishing words together.

"How'd you do that?" he asks.

"Stuff like that? That's what elephants do. Over and over, until there's no wobble."

Africa's skull sinks. "Not all elephants," he says.

Zoo drags and kicks her keys, clock, and water bottle a half acre closer to Africa. Then she shares her most pressing concern. "The zoo's about to close for renovations. And I'm too sick and dangerous. No one wants me. Or the big fuzzy cranky neighbor that lives in the middle of the zoo."

"The polar bear?" he asks.

"Yup. If people can't find a place for us? Well. You know. It's lights out."

"That's why we sent help. The new night handler is your ticket out of your cage," Africa says.

"All the new guys stop showing up," Zoo says.

"Not this one. He'll be with you every night, no matter your mood."

Africa tests the tree trunk to see if it can endure a full-on back scratch. The elm rustles and takes his weight. "He is family. He's been trying to find you. For twenty winters. Do you trust him?"

"Sure," Zoo says.

"Yes or no?" Africa asks.

"Sure. I mean, yes, I trust him. He baked me cookies. Dry as! But way better than oat brick. *Cookie* is my favorite word." She gathers her metal and plastic objects and clambers over to within twenty feet of Africa.

"What has he asked you to do?"

"To eat. And something about getting in a good workout," she says.

Zoo dives into a pre-workout stretch.

"What is this peculiar thing you are doing?" he asks.

Africa's magnificent shadow distracts her. It takes Zoo a minute to respond. She mumbles from an uncomfortable inverted position. "What? This? Stretching."

Zoo snaps back to a flirtatious upright posture— way too fast. "Whoa! Head rush." She puts a bony foot on a boulder for an utterly useless lower-leg stretch. She has a crush on Africa. It makes her nervous. Performance mode takes over. Zoo stands on one leg.

"This is the most advanced move of all," she says.

It's a struggle to balance without the sensitive fleshy foot cushion. But she also realizes that she's free of pain from the foot disorders common among captive elephants.

"It's a little hard to hold position. But, hey, at least it doesn't hurt. Sometimes I worry."

"What is one thing you worry about?" Africa asks.

"That I get kind of scrambled. In my head. And there's lots of stuff I don't remember. And I can't count past two anymore. And I rock back and forth. And why don't I have any friends? I rumble. But no reply."

"We hear you." Africa refocuses Zoo's attention with a grounding question. "When you stand on one foot, what does it do?"

"People like it," she says.

He scans the meadow. "No people here."

* * *

Sunlight beams off bent-aluminum elephant cookie cutters. About three dozen of them collide and bonk around as they organize into approximate exercise rows. Zoo is scared.

"Those guys look like trouble," she says.

"They are good guys. It's all cookies on deck for a friend. Time for the workout. You are in charge," Africa says.

"Me? In charge? No way."

The elephant cookie cutters wait until Zoo figures out a resolution to the awkward silence. She starts to march in place. Then she practices leadership skills.

"On two," she says. "Here we go. Ready?" Zoo's voice falters. "One. Two."

All recently assembled aluminum workout buddies straggle off in different directions. Africa rumbles a command and they regroup. Zoo is impressed. "Look at that! All lined up and ready for instructions. Okay. Here we go. On two. Ready. One. Two!" The elephants wiggle.

Zoo adds a layer of physiological technique. "Really work it! You know. Like this! Get those feet up." The elephant cookie cutters have poorly defined limbs. Low-frequency sound waves move through the group. Zoo recognizes that sound. "Infrasonic. Nice," she says.

A headset with a microphone appears, and then a speaker. Zoo tests the portable audio system. "Check. Check. Check one, two. Welcome to the workout zone. Yikes. Reverb. That came out super weird." The noise disturbs the group. They contract into a herd formation. Zoo ditches the headset.

A boom box appears. Zoo's psyched. She presses play but the music is too loud. She struggles with the miniscule volume knob. The perfect workout song starts, first with a little intro synthesizer, and then it kicks into gear. The elephants cardio-march in place. Zoo tries to keep the energy up. "Here we go. Ready for lunges? On two. Lunges on two. One. Two!" The workout music revs up, and the group drops it down for a short session of high-intensity lunges.

Zoo calls for a break. "Good job. Puff it out. Recovery." The elephants are wrecked. They did not enjoy lunges. Zoo chucks her water bottle over to Africa. It lands at his feet.

"What is this?" he asks.

"It's a water bottle. Don't even. Come on. For real? Even when you were little? You never used a bottle?"

Africa's voice comes through the boom box. In his best effort at synthy vocals, he asks a mind-blowing question. "How do you feel?"

"How do I feel?" Zoo's skeleton explodes, catches an updraft, then scrunches into a ball and crashes to the ground. "Not good. I'm all over the place. And lunges kick my ass. Big time."

"Collect yourself," Africa commands. Zoo obeys. She reassembles and basks in the crystalline sunlight.

Africa does a three-sixty. He's back with an accessory.

"Nice sweatband," Zoo says.

Africa does another three-sixty and returns with a fake moustache. He tilts his head to form a plateau. "I cannot get this thing to stick," he says. With a bizarre hairy slide down his weathered skull, the moustache falls. It entangles in his digits as he tries to sweep it away.

"Sweet 'stache," Zoo says.

"Lucky. Us drifters," Africa says. The elephant cookie cutters make a decent effort to wave. "Home is anywhere. Call on us anytime. We are up for anything." The elephant cookie cutters sway. "Correction. Anything except lunges."

"I live on the other side of the eight-hundred-acre park. Wow! Eight hundred, how'd I remember that number?" Zoo asks.

"Nothing beats a good workout," Africa says.

"Want to see my house?" Zoo collects her water bottle, clock and keys.

"Let's walk the neighborhoods instead. Once around the park. Leave your things."

* * *

Neighborhood by neighborhood, unhurried, Africa and Zoo stroll the park's perimeter. They start at the Upper East Side, Harlem, Upper West Side, counter clockwise, around they go. It gets darker. Finally, the elephant skeletons approach the Central Zoo maintenance entrance. Africa glows, then disappears. Zoo is alone outside the locked gate.

Zoo disassembles. The smallest bones are silent as they filter through the bars. Some pieces clank on the steel. Her scattered body drifts through the zoo, passing caged exotics in variable states of unrest. Most of the exhibits are already empty in preparation for the zoo closing for major renovations. She gives the polar bear a hug. When she arrives at the elephant barn, she collapses into a pile of bones.

CPSIA information can be obtained
at www.ICGtesting.com
Printed in the USA
BVHW07s2226280518
517560BV00003B/477/P